Pancakes

Written by Jo Windsor
Illustrated by Clive Taylor

Rigby

Nell loves to cook.
She is the greatest cook
in the world.

"Come to breakfast, Pete,"
she called.
"We will have pancakes.
I'll show you how
to make them."

3

4

Nell and Pete
ate the pancakes.
"Yum," they said.
"Pancakes are good to eat.
We like pancakes."

Dad came in.
"Ah!" he said.
"Pancakes for breakfast.
I'll make pancakes, too.
I like pancakes.
They are good to eat."

7

Uncle Jack came in.
"Oh, good," he said.
"Pancakes for breakfast.
Pancakes are good to eat."

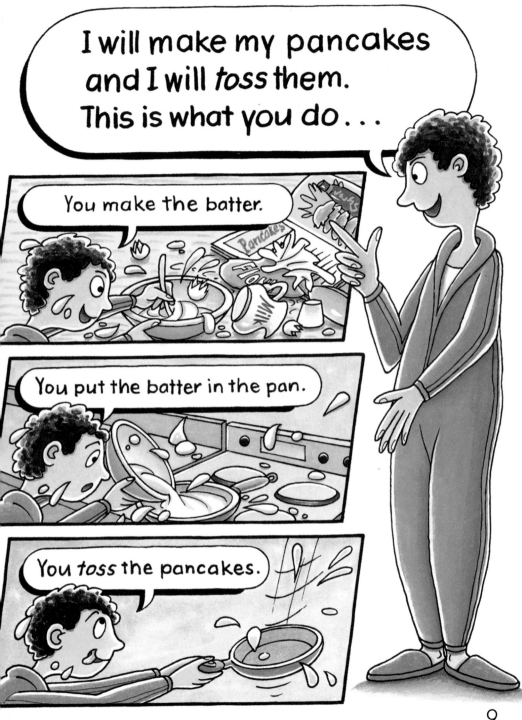

9

Uncle Jack tossed the pancake. The pancake went up, up, up. "My pancake!" he shouted. "Where is my pancake?" He looked up.

"Oh, dear!" said Uncle Jack.
"Look at my pancake!"
And then,
down came the pancake
on top of his head.

"Oh well," said Uncle Jack.
"Birds love pancakes."
And he tossed the pancake out.

A Recipe

Pancakes

You will need:
 1 cup flour
 1 cup milk
 1 egg
Put the flour into a bowl.

Put in the egg and the milk. Mix.

Get Mom or Dad to help you cook the pancakes in the hot pan.

▬▬ Guide Notes

Title: Pancakes
Stage: Early (3) – Blue

Genre: Fiction
Approach: Guided Reading
Processes: Thinking Critically, Exploring Language, Processing Information
Written and Visual Focus: Recipe

THINKING CRITICALLY
(sample questions)
- What do you think this story could be about?
- What do you know about making pancakes?
- If you were going to make a pancake, what would you need?
- Look at page 5. How do you know Nell and Pete like pancakes?
- Look at page 6. What do you think Dad could be saying?
- Look at pages 12 and 13. Why do you think the pancake went up on the ceiling?
- What else do you think Uncle Jack could have done with his pancake?

EXPLORING LANGUAGE

Terminology
Title, cover, illustrations, author, illustrator

Vocabulary
Interest words: pancakes, greatest, mixture, tossed, flip
High-frequency words (new): show, head, breakfast, how, uncle
Positional words: up, down, top, over
Compound word: pancakes

Print Conventions
Capital letter for sentence beginnings and names (**Nell**, **Pete**, **Uncle Tom**, **Dad**), periods, exclamation marks, quotation marks, commas, ellipses, question marks